W9-DCF-046

Rainbow Fish & Friends

SOS

SAVE OUR SHORTCUT!

TEXT BY GAIL DONOVAN
ILLUSTRATIONS BY DAVID AUSTIN CLAR STUDIO

Night Sky Books
New York · London

Rainbow Fish and his friends were late for school.

"Shortcut time!" shouted Spike. "Bet you can't cut through crabby Mrs. Crabbitz's sculptures without touching a single rock!"

"Not a wise move," warned Dyna.

"I agree," said Rusty. "I don't want to be late, but I don't want to get in trouble, either."

"Oh, come on!" said Rainbow Fish. "We won't hurt anything!"

They were halfway through when Mrs. Crabbitz scuttled out. "You slippery little fish! I've told you a hundred times not to cut through here! Now, I've caught you knocking over my sculptures." She pointed to a pile of fallen rocks and shells.

"But, we didn't touch a thing," said Rainbow Fish. "Honest!"

"Hmph!" she snapped. "You're just like these pesky plants I keep pulling up. Always making a mess of my garden. Now, shoo!"

"Oh, no! Late for school and in trouble, too," said Rusty. "Maybe we *did* make the rocks fall down."

Dyna reassured him. "The chances of that are very slim."

"I wish I *had* knocked them over," Spike said. "I don't like being yelled at for something I didn't do."

"Me neither," said Rainbow Fish.

"Attention, fish," said Miss Cuttle. "Our garden needs weeding this morning."

"Hooray!" shouted Spike. "No classes!"

"The garden is our classroom, too," said Miss Cuttle. "Now, remember, think before you pull, and pull gently. We don't want to take everything out of the garden—just what the garden doesn't need."

"I'm weeding seaweed. I'm weeding seaweed," Little Blue sang over and over as he pulled plants from the garden. He tugged on a stubborn strand. When it finally came out, he went flying into Angel.

"Watch it!" she said. "You're getting dirt all over me!"

"I can't help it," said Little Blue. "I'm weeding seaweed."

"You're also weeding plants we want to keep!" cried Angel. "You don't have to pull up the whole reef!"

The walls around Little Blue's section of the garden
began to tumble in.

"Cave-in!" shouted Spike. "Alert! Alert! Landslide!"

"Check it out," said Rainbow Fish. "It looks just like Mrs.
Crabbitz's garden!"

"That's it!" cried Dyna. "Pulling up too many plants can
loosen the soil. That must be why her sculptures fall down!"

Everyone pitched in and helped rebuild the garden. But when they were done, they found they had one big beautiful shell left over from the border.

"Oh, dear. It isn't exactly the way it was before," said Rusty.

"It's okay, Rusty. I think it looks even better," said Rainbow Fish. "Besides, I know someone who might be able to use this."

After school, Rainbow Fish led Dyna, Spike, and Rusty back to Mrs. Crabbitz's garden.

"I'm not so sure this is a good idea," muttered Rusty. "What if she yells at us again?"

Rainbow Fish wasn't looking forward to that, either. But
he knew they had to tell Mrs. Crabbitz what they'd learned.
"Hello!" he called. "Anybody home?"

"How many times do I have to tell you . . . ," yelled Mrs. Crabbitz.

"We're sorry we cut through before," said Rainbow Fish. "We thought this might look nice in your garden."

"Hmph!" snapped Mrs. Crabbitz. "A lot of good that will do. My garden's already ruined."

Rainbow Fish wanted to leave right then, but he didn't give up. Instead, he told her about the landslide that had happened in their own garden.

"Hmph," she said again. "I've got work to do. Now move along."

A few days later Rainbow Fish and his friends swam by Mrs. Crabbitz's sculpture garden.

"Look!" Dyna whispered, "It's a metamorphosis."

"A what?" asked Spike.

"A big change," explained Dyna.

"Yes it is! Now it's a perfect shortcut!" said Rainbow Fish, and he took off with the others right behind him.

Mrs. Crabbitz scuttled right into their path. "Not so fast! Stop right there!"

"We're sorry, Mrs. Crabbitz," said Rainbow Fish. "We couldn't resist coming in. Your garden is so beautiful!"

"Hmph!" she snapped. "Then don't swim so fast, and you'll see it better. And stick to the path. My plants are still taking root. You can look, but don't touch!"

"What a crab!" said Spike.

"Really," said Dyna. "No metamorphosis there."

"I guess some things never change," said Rainbow Fish. "She's still the same old Mrs. Crabbitz. But that's okay with me."